BARNEY IS BEST

Nancy White Carlstrom
Illustrated by James Graham Hale

■ HarperCollins*Publishers*

Library of Congress Cataloging-in-Publication Data
Carlstrom, Nancy White.
 Barney is best /Nancy White Carlstrom ; illustrated by James Graham Hale.
  p.   cm.
 Summary: A child going to the hospital to have tonsils removed insists on
bringing a worn but beloved stuffed animal instead of a newer one.
 ISBN 0-06-022875-X. — ISBN 0-06-022876-8 (lib. bdg.)
 [1. Toys—Fiction. 2. Hospitals—Fiction. 3. Hispanic Americans—
Fiction.] I. Hale, James Graham, ill. II. Title.
PZ7.C21684Bar   1994   92-30376
[E]—dc20   CIP
                                                              AC

2   3   4   5   6   7   8   9   10

For my brother Jim, Dr. Carol, Becca, and Nathan,
With love,
—N.W.C.

Tomorrow
I have to go
to the hospital.

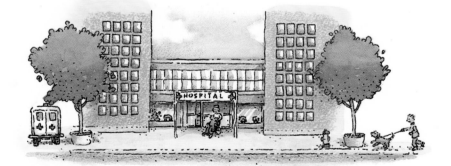

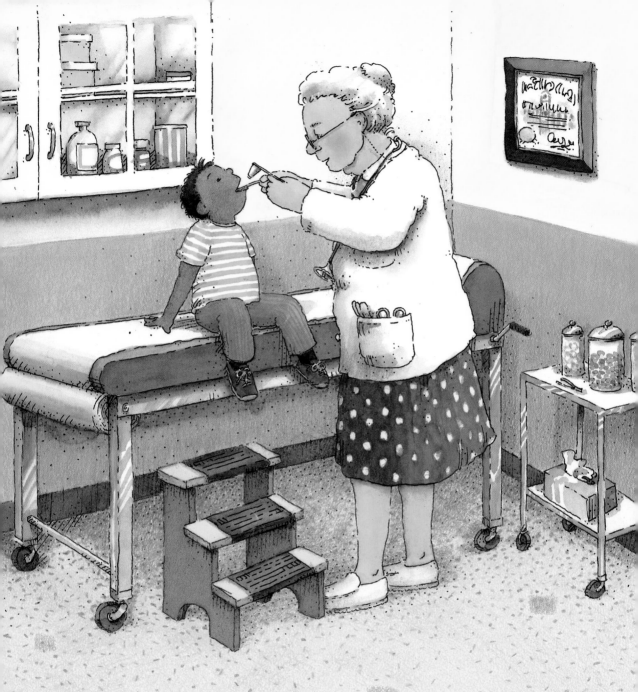

Dr. Johnson says they need
to take out my tonsils.

She says everything will be okay.
But I'm still scared.

Mama says, "It's okay to feel scared.
But you won't be alone. We'll be there.
And you can take one
of your stuffed animals, too!"

Papa says, "Take Benito!"
My brother Daniel says, "Take Coco!"

I think about it.

Benito is soft and fluffy
and has a shiny black nose.

Coco's eyes really move
and he smells brand new.

I leave them both sitting on my bed
in the morning.

Every night they are waiting for me.
Right where I left them.

But Barney is best.
I want to take Barney.

"Not Barney," Mama says.
"He's had too many spins
in the washing machine.

He has to wear a Band-Aid
to keep his stuffing in."

"But when we were camping last summer
and I couldn't get to sleep,

Daniel let Barney stay in my sleeping bag.
Remember?
Barney was better than a pillow."

"I remember," Mama says.
Barney is best.

"Not Barney," Papa says.
"His eyes don't match
and he smells like a worn-out shoe."

"But when we went to the airport
and I left my dinosaur book in the car
and we couldn't go back,
Daniel let me carry Barney
to the airplane. Remember?

Barney has X-ray eyes.
Even better than that machine
he went through."

"I remember," Papa says.
Barney is best.

"Not Barney," says Daniel.
"He won't stay where you put him.
He'll do somersaults on your pillow
and flop off your bed."

"But when you went to kindergarten
and I cried 'cause I wanted to go too,
you said I could play with Barney.
Remember?

All morning Barney made me laugh
with his tricks."

"I remember," Daniel says.
Barney is best.

"And even when I was born,
you brought Barney out to meet me
at the hospital.
Remember?"

"We remember!"

"Better take Barney to the hospital,"
Daniel says.
"He's been there before!"

Don't worry, Barney!

Everything is going to be okay!